From the Land
of Serendipity™...

your own
keepsakc
bookmark.

PRICE STERN SLOAN
Los Angeles

Fanny

Written and illustrated
by Robin James

A Serendipity™ Book

PRICE STERN SLOAN
Los Angeles

ISBN: 0-8431-1460-6

Serendipity ™ and The Pink Dragon ® are trademarks of Price Stern Sloan, Inc.

28 27 26 25 24

Dedicated to my dearest of dear friends, Susan Malarky and Patti Kelly. They showed me that being handicapped is a state of mind.

Stephen

Beside a long, dusty road far out in the country was a lonely old wooden fence. The fence stood alone for miles and miles with only sweet-smelling lilac and an occasional honeysuckle rose for companions.

At the very end of the rickity picket fence was an old run-down farm nestled at the top of a wooded hill. The farm was filled with all sorts of animals: tough old chickens who laid very few eggs, some tough old cows who gave very little milk, and a small herd of tough old sheep who gave very little wool at all.

Amidst the animals of this old barnyard lived a fluffy, grey cat named Fanny. In many ways Fanny was an ordinary cat. She had an ordinary long, swishy tail like all other cats. She had ordinary green eyes that looked at all the world in wonder like all other cats. Ordinary, yes, but different too, for Fanny had only three legs.

Because Fanny had only three legs instead of four she had to hobble and hop to and fro to get to there and back again. She hopped to get a drink of milk and on warm spring days, hopped atop the fence to sun herself. Even though she had only three legs Fanny got around pretty well. In fact, she needed no help from any of the other animals in the barnyard — not that they had ever offered any.

The other animals never talked to Fanny because they felt it was too embarrassing to talk to a creature who was handicapped.

Whenever Fanny hobbled by the chickens would turn their backs, ruffle their feathers and look the other way. Sometimes a chick would try to talk to her, but one of the old hens would always come kickling and cackling and shoo the chick away. "Don't talk to her little chick-chick. You would just embarrass her. Besides, she has nothing to say." But Fanny would act as if she didn't mind and hobble on her way.

Whenever she hopped by the dairy barn all of the cows would gawk and stare with big, brown, blinking eyes as she passed. If one of the calves tried to stick its neck through the fence to talk to her, one of the old, bossy milk cows would moo it away and say, "Don't stare, you silly calf. You'll just embarrass her. Besides, she has nothing to say." Fanny would just pretend she didn't hear as she batted at a bumblebee or butterfly that happened to be flying by.

Whenever Fanny took the well-worn path in the pasture between the barn and the old farmhouse, the little spring lambs would gather to talk to her as she limped by. No sooner would they start rushing through the clover than an old ewe would call them back to the flock. "Come back little lambs and don't be bad! You'll just embarrass her. Besides, she has nothing to say."

Poor, old Fanny would just continue on her way.

So, none of the creatures would talk to Fanny as she went quietly on her way. None, that is, except for a scruffy little puppy named Ruby. Little Ruby had no parents that anyone could remember and slept in an old building filled with hay.

Ruby loved to kiss and lick the other animals of the farm. With each one of the creatures it was the same: kisses and licks, kisses and licks. It was often said that Ruby was the fastest licker around.

With tail wagging, she would sidle up to a chicken with sleep still in its eyes and before that chicken could let out a cackle, her tongue was out, the lick was licked and it would squawk, "Oh, yuuck! Oh, me! Oh, my!"

Well, all the animals had been licked and loved by Ruby so much that one day an old ewe and a bossy cow cruelly dared the little puppy to kiss old Fanny as she hobbled on her way.

Ruby took the dare, and hiding in the tall clover that grew by the fence, she waited for the cat to come by. Sure enough, in no time at all old Fanny came hobbling along. With a leap and a giggle Ruby dashed from the clover and gave Fanny a long and loving lick from the tip of her nose to the top of her head. That little dog surely was the fastest licker around.

Old Fanny didn't try to run away like the other animals. Instead, she just licked and loved that scruffy puppy right back, lick for lick. Contrary to what the barnyard animals had thought, Fanny wasn't embarrassed in the slightest and she had *a lot* to say.

Ruby and Fanny sat on that path for the longest of times just licking and loving and laughing about this and that. Later, in the old wooden barn, they curled up together in a warm pile of hay. As the sun peeked through the cracks and slats they fell fast asleep, curled up in each other's love.

From that day forward the two of them were thought of as one, for they shared all the farm had to share. Together they hobbled and hopped from here to there and back again. They stopped at the chicken pens and talked to the chicks about the weather, and chatted about the sunflowers that grew so very tall. The chicks were shocked to find that Fanny wasn't embarrassed by her handicap at all; she had a lot to say!

They chatted with the calves at the dairy barn. The calves were so moved by what Fanny had to say that they shared some milk they had gotten from the old bossy cow (who just looked the other way). That cat mewed and meowed loudly so that all could hear about her life on the farm, a tale she had never been able to share before.

Fanny and Ruby walked through the meadow of deep purple clover talking to the lambs as they frolicked and played. And they, too, learned that she had a heart full of things she wanted to say.

From that day forward the lambs, the calves, the chicks, a scruffy little puppy named Ruby and a handicapped, three-legged cat named Fanny were the best of friends. For Fanny had never been handicapped by what she was, only by what the other creatures thought she was.

AS YOU WALK, HOP, HOBBLE, OR WHEEL
MEETING PEOPLE OF DIFFERENT KINDS,
REMEMBER THAT BEING HANDICAPPED
IS ONLY A STATE OF MIND.

ℰerendipity™ ℬooks

Created by Stephen Cosgrove and Robin James

Enjoy all the delightful books in the Serendipity™ Series:

The above books, and many others, can be bought wherever books are sold, or may be ordered directly from the publisher.
Call toll-free: (800) 631-8571

PRICE STERN SLOAN
Customer Service Department
390 Murray Hill Parkway, East Rutherford, NJ 07073